Chris Powling

Sharks

Illustrated by Rupert van Wyk

OXFORD
UNIVERSITY PRESS

This book belongs to

OXFORD
UNIVERSITY PRESS

Great Clarendon Street, Oxford OX2 6DP

Oxford University Press is a department of the University of Oxford.
It furthers the University's objective of excellence in research, scholarship,
and education by publishing worldwide in

Oxford New York

Athens Auckland Bangkok Bogotá Buenos Aires Calcutta
Cape Town Chennai Dar es Salaam Delhi Florence Hong Kong Istanbul
Karachi Kuala Lumpur Madrid Melbourne Mexico City Mumbai
Nairobi Paris São Paulo Singapore Taipei Tokyo Toronto Warsaw

Oxford is a registered trade mark of Oxford University Press
in the UK and in certain other countries

Text copyright © Chris Powling 2000
Illustrations copyright © Rupert van Wyk 2000

The moral rights of the author and artist have been asserted

First published 2000

Paperback ISBN 0-19-910623-1
Pack of 6 ISBN 0-19-910757-2
Pack of 36 ISBN 0-19-910758-0

This edition is also available in Oxford Reading Tree
Branch Library Stages 8-10 Pack A

3 5 7 9 10 8 6 4

Printed and bound in Spain by Edelvives

Contents

▶ Sharks can be scary

Even a shark's name makes me
shiver.
It seems to be saying:

SH – to hush us

AR – to swallow us

K – to snap shut on us!

Grey reef shark

Sharks haven't changed for millions of years. They're like leftover dinosaurs.

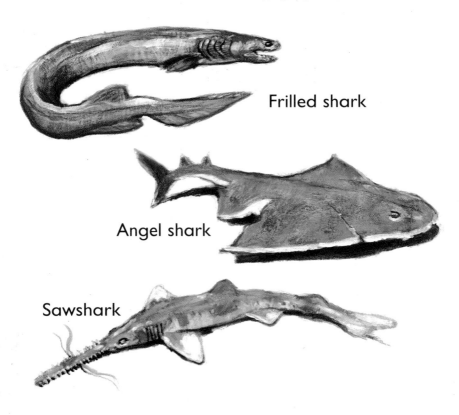

Frilled shark

Angel shark

Sawshark

Do sharks ever sleep? No.
Do sharks ever stop swimming? No.
Do sharks ever feel afraid? No.

We can say no to all these questions,
at least if we're talking about the
scariest shark of all. From the
colour of its belly, we call this the
Great White.

▶ The Great White

When it's a thousand metres away,
a Great White will hear you.

When it's five hundred metres away,
it'll smell you.

When it's a hundred metres away,
it'll notice the splash of your feet in
the water.

Imagine being hunted by an animal that's bigger and faster than a speedboat.

What a nightmare!

Great White shark

This shark's bite is the worst part.
A Great White can gulp down a
whole seal in one go. Its teeth are so
sharp you won't even feel them
slicing into you … at first.

▶ Other sorts of shark

Most sharks are more friendly. Look at the Whale shark ...

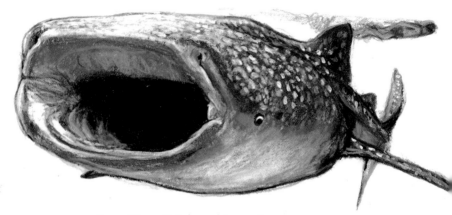

... or the Basking shark.

These are the biggest fish in the sea. Amazingly, neither will harm you.

They're too busy feeding themselves.
They spend hour after hour
hoovering up tiny fish and plants.
They won't even mind if you sneak
a ride with them.

A Dwarf shark, though, could sneak
a ride with you. It's the smallest
shark there is.

So far, we know about more than 350 different kinds of shark. Some are so strange, they seem almost magical. It's hard to believe in the Zebra shark …

… or the Carpet shark,

… or the Thresher shark.

The Goblin shark
is stranger still …

… and so is the
Horn shark.

Strangest of all, perhaps, is the
Wobbegong.

Can they all be sharks when they
look so different?

▶ How to recognize a shark

1. Check the mouth

On a shark the
mouth is tucked
under the snout.
It opens much wider
than your mouth
or mine.

2. Check the teeth

Inside the mouth are
hundreds of teeth –
for gripping, for
crushing, for slicing.
When a tooth falls
out, another shifts
forward to take
its place.

3. Check the gills

Gills are hidden slits which help fish breathe underwater. On sharks, the gills *aren't* hidden. A shark has a set of five gills on each side of its throat.

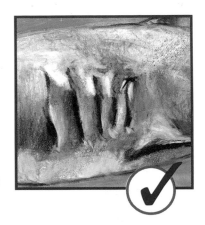

4. Check the skin ... very gently

Fish have scales but sharks are covered in tiny, tooth-like thorns called denticles. These are amazingly sharp. Stroke them one way and they'll be as smooth as silk. Stroke them the other and your fingers may gush with blood.

5. Check the skeleton

A shark's skeleton isn't bony. It's made of gristly stuff known as cartilage, just like your nose and your ears. That's why a shark can twist and turn so easily.

6. Check a couple of shark secrets

One is the special oil in a shark's liver that helps keep it afloat.

The other is a long, thin tube, filled with jelly. This loops from snout to tail inside a shark's body. It twangs if there's any movement in the water. Its name is the lateral line.

▶ Are sharks really dangerous?

Well, you'd better stay on the beach
if there's a Great White lurking
about.

Or the Blue shark which swims in
packs. Or the Hammerhead …
the Mako … or the Tiger shark.

Great White

Blue shark

All five are sleek, skilful hunters.
Mostly they kill seals, sea lions and
turtles.

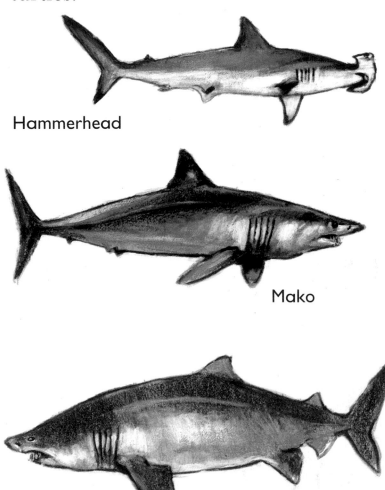

Hammerhead

Mako

Tiger shark

But sharks also kill people, don't they?

Only by mistake, most experts say. Sharks are so bold and so hungry, they gobble down almost anything – tin cans, old tools, plastic bags. To them, a boy or girl on a surfboard may look just like a seal or a turtle.

Remember, too, that a shark attack is very rare. There are sharks all over the world wherever the sea is warm. Yet, every year, the number of people they bite wouldn't even fill a classroom in your school.

Did you know ...
More people are
struck by lightning
than bitten by sharks!

A shark's worst enemy

This may surprise you. Human beings are far more deadly to sharks than sharks are to us!

 We hunt them for sport.

We turn their teeth into necklaces.

We use their skin for shoes and wallets and handbags.

We crush their skeleton for plant food.

We even take the oil in their liver for making perfume and face cream and soap.

BAMBOO PALACE MENU

Supreme Broth
Tiger Sharkfin Soup
Dark Chicken Sharkfin Soup
Crab Meat Sharkfin Soup
Boiled Dried Seafood Deluxe
Roast Duck in Plum Sauce
Squid in Black Bean Sauce
Steamed Vegetables with
Oyster Sauce
Egg Fried Rice
Jasmine Tea

Also, we eat them ... in sharkfin soup
for starters and as steaks for a main
course. If you like fish and chips,
watch out for "huss" or "rock
salmon" on the menu. Its real name
is the dogfish. And that's a small
shark.

▶ The vanishing shark

Sharks are beginning to disappear.

Nowadays we kill sharks much faster than they can breed. In fact, we don't know much about how sharks have babies. Or how often it happens.

Some sharks lay eggs in a special case called a Mermaid's purse.

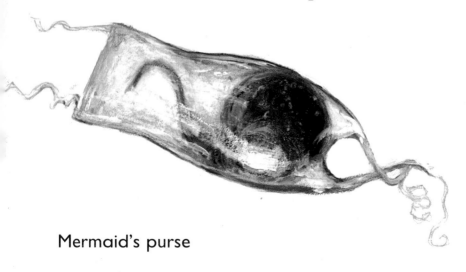

Mermaid's purse

Other sharks are hatched inside their mother. A Lemon shark is different again – it gives birth to a pup that's nearly as big as a man.

These babies have always been easy food for bigger sea creatures.

Eventually, if we're not careful, there may not be any sharks left in the sea.

Think about that.

Lemon shark and pup

Do we really want sharks to die out altogether just like dinosaurs?

Of course, I wouldn't want a shark as a pet. Would you? But I'd love to discover more about them. How much food do they really eat, for instance? And how long do they live? Even shark experts can't answer these questions yet.

Great White sharks

Maybe we should find a new way of saying their name. Why not try:

SH – to concentrate

 **AR** – to admire

K – to click the camera for a close-up.

That should do it!

Greenland shark

Leopard shark

Bull shark

Lemon shark

Sharks still send a shiver up my spine.
But I hope these mysterious creatures
will always be there to scare us and
thrill us.

▶ Glossary

 breed When sharks breed they produce babies. **24**

 cartilage Sharks have a skeleton made of tough but elastic material called cartilage. **16**

 denticles Denticles are the little sharp scales that cover a shark's body. **15**

 gills Gills are the long thin slits behind a shark's head. The shark uses them to breathe through. **15**

lateral line The lateral line is a long, thin tube, filled with jelly. This loops from snout to tail inside a shark's body. It twangs if there's any movement in the water. **17**

 mermaid's purse Some sharks lay their eggs in a mermaid's purse. It is a little bag that protects a shark's eggs. **24**

 pup A pup is a baby shark. **25**

 snout A snout is the pointed "nose" in front of a shark's eyes. **14, 17**

Reading Together

Oxford Reds have been written by leading children's authors who have a passion for particular non-fiction subjects. So as well as up-to-date information, fascinating facts and stunning pictures, these books provide powerful writing which draws the reader into the text.

Oxford Reds are written in simple language, checked by educational advisors. There is plenty of repetition of words and phrases, and all technical words are explained. They are an ideal vehicle for helping your child develop a love of reading – by building fluency, confidence and enjoyment.

You can help your child by reading the first few pages out loud, then encourage him or her to continue alone. You could share the reading by taking turns to read a page or two. Or you could read the whole book aloud, so your child knows it well before tackling it alone.

Oxford Reds will help your child develop a love of reading and a lasting curiosity about the world we live in.

Sue Palmer
Writer and Literacy Consultant